P9-CPV-187

Silver Seeds

A book of nature poems

by **Paul Paolilli** and **Dan Brewer**

paintings by **Steve Johnson** and **Lou Fancher**

VIKING

Down goes the moon

And up comes the sun,

Welcoming the

New day.

d   a

SUN

Sliding through the window,

Underneath the door,

Nudging us out to play.

Silent friend

Holding onto our heels

And

Drawing our picture

On the ground

With black crayon.

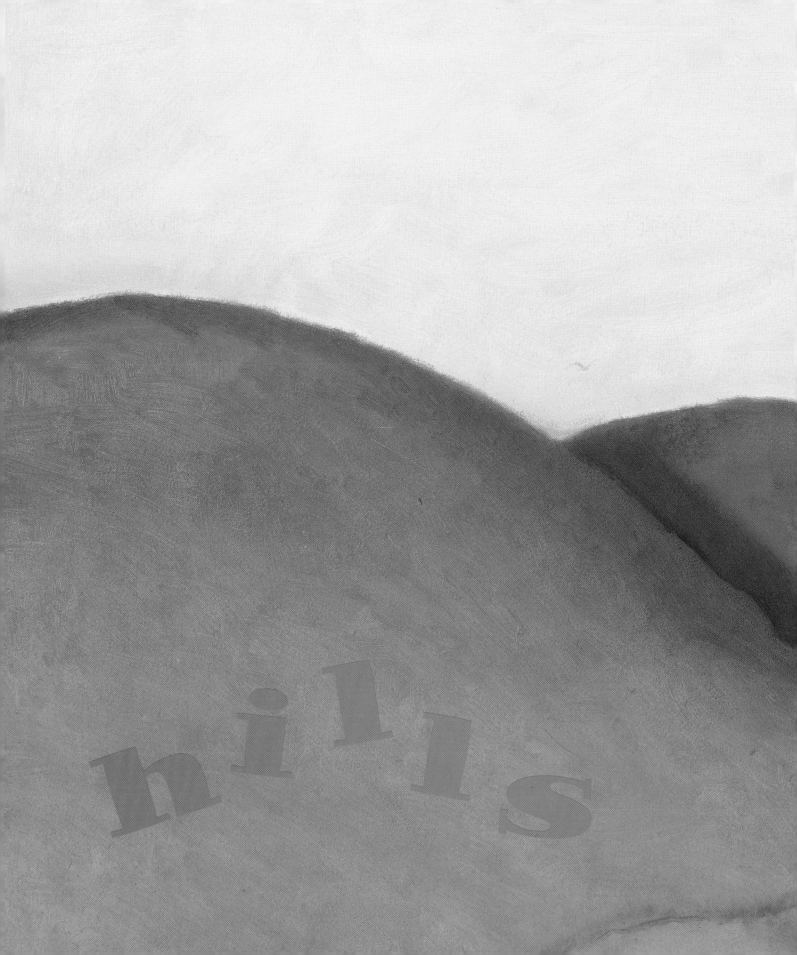

hills

Huge elephants

In a row,

Lying

Low and

Sleeping.

Tiny hands

Reaching up from the

Earth, tickling an

Enormous

Sky.

Trees

Loose brown parachute

Escaping

And

Floating on puffs of air.

Bzzzzzzz…

Echoes in our

Ears.

bee

Bobbing

Up and down;

Twinkling

Through the air

Ever so gently,

Roaming among the

Flowers,

Landing lightly on

Your shoulder.

but

Humming

bird

Hovering

Under the

Morning glories,

Moving back and forth on

Invisible wings,

Neatly sipping nectar,

Going from

Blossom to blossom

In

Rapid

Darts and dashes.

d   s

Creamy scoops of ice cream

Lying

Out

Under a

Dreamy blue

Sky.

f

Folds and folds

Of spun sugar, like a soft

Gray blanket over the land.

Rap-tap-tapping

At my window

In drip-drop

Notes.

Marvelous melon, whole

Or sliced,

Offering sweet flavor to the

Night.

m o o n

Silver seeds

Tossed in the air

And planted in the sky,

Reaching out of the darkness

Sprouting wonder.

Night

Now it

Is time to

Gather our dreams,

Holding them tight

Till tomorrow comes.

To Sue, Chris and Dena, who fill my heart— P. P.

To my wife, Linda, who every day brings me joy— D. B.

For Michelle, Garrett and Colin— S. J. & L. F.

VIKING
Published by the Penguin Group
Penguin Putnam Books for Young Readers, 345 Hudson Street, New York, New York 10014, U.S.A.
Penguin Books Ltd, 27 Wrights Lane, London W8 5TZ, England
Penguin Books Australia Ltd, Ringwood, Victoria, Australia
Penguin Books Canada Ltd, 10 Alcorn Avenue, Toronto, Ontario, Canada M4V 3B2
Penguin Books (N.Z.) Ltd, 182-190 Wairau Road, Auckland 10, New Zealand

Penguin Books Ltd, Registered Offices: Harmondsworth, Middlesex, England

First published in 2001 by Viking, a division of Penguin Putnam Books for Young Readers.

1   3   5   7   9   10   8   6   4   2

Library of Congress Cataloging-in-Publication Data

Paolilli, Paul.
Silver seeds : a book of nature poems / by Paul Paolilli and Dan
Brewer ; illustrated by Steve Johnson and Lou Fancher.
p.   cm.
ISBN 0-670-88941-5
1. Nature—Juvenile poetry. 2. Children's poetry, American. [1.
Nature—Poetry. 2. American poetry.] I. Brewer, Dan. II. Johnson,
Steve, 1960- ill. III. Fancher, Lou, ill. IV. Title.
PS3566.A5943 S55 2001
811'.6—dc21
00-009469

Printed in Hong Kong
Set in Garamond and other assorted fonts

Book design by Lou Fancher